Written and illustrated by Adam Hargreaves

MR. MEN LITTLE MISS

PSS!
PRICE STERN SLOAN
An Imprint of Penguin Group (USA) Inc.

 First published in the United States in 2007 by Price Stern Sloan, a division of Penguin Young Readers Group, 345 Hudson Street, New York, New York 10014. *PSS!* is a registered trademark of Penguin Group (USA) Inc. Manufactured in the U.S.A.

ISBN 978-0-8431-2130-8 10 9

The very best thing about birthdays, as far as Mr. Birthday is concerned, is birthday parties.

Cards are nice, presents are good, but parties are great.

Mr. Birthday likes birthday parties so much that he is never without his party hat!

". . . *your* birthday!"

"Happy birthday, Mr. Birthday!" cried all of Mr. Birthday's friends.

Mr. Birthday blushed. "How silly of me," he said.

And Mr. Birthday is very good at organizing birthday parties. He likes to make sure that everyone he knows has a party on their birthday.

In just the last three weeks, he has organized a party with two cakes for Mr. Greedy.

One cake for all the guests and one for Mr. Greedy!

A party with silly hats for Mr. Silly because . . .

. . . Mr. Silly is silly!

And a party with no balloons for Mr. Jelly because Mr. Jelly is scared of balloons . . .

. . . in case they go POP!

POP!

This week, Mr. Birthday organized a very happy birthday party for Mr. Happy.

He invited all of Mr. Happy's friends, including Little Miss Sunshine, Mr. Funny, Little Miss Lucky, and Mr. Bump.

Mr. Birthday put up lots of balloons and a big banner saying **"Happy Birthday, Mr. Happy!"**

And he organized fun party games for everyone to play.

Happy Birthday, Mr Happy!

Little Miss Lucky won hot potato.

And then she won pin the tail on the donkey.

She is not called Little Miss Lucky for nothing!

It was difficult to know who won musical chairs
because Mr. Bump kept knocking over the chairs.

After the party games, Mr. Birthday brought in a huge birthday cake. Mr. Happy smiled an extra wide smile and blew out all the candles in one try!

Then they all ate a feast of birthday cake, jam sandwiches, Jell-O, and ice cream.

Everyone had a wonderful time.

When the party had finished, Mr. Happy thanked Mr. Birthday.

"We mustn't forget that extra special birthday next week," added Mr. Happy with a wink as he said good-bye.

Mr. Birthday racked his brains as he walked home.

"I wonder whose birthday Mr. Happy was talking about," he puzzled.

But try as he might, no one came to mind.

He looked in his diary when he reached home, but there was no one's birthday written in for the next week.

"Mr. Happy must have got it wrong," he reassured himself as he got into bed.

But the next day, Mr. Birthday kept overhearing things that seemed to suggest there really was a very important birthday coming up.

He passed Mr. Worry in the street.

"Oh my! Oh gosh! What ever am I going to buy as a present for next week?" muttered Mr. Worry to himself. "What a worry!"

He overheard Mr. Forgetful who was repeating, "I must not forget the party next week, I must not forget the party next week, I must not forget the party next week," over and over to himself.

"I must not forget the . . ." he said and stopped mid-sentence. Then he looked at his hand, ". . . the party! I must not forget the party next week."

Poor Mr. Birthday was distraught. How could there be a birthday, and a birthday party, he knew nothing about?

Party

The following day, he decided that he would just have to go and ask Mr. Happy.

Mr. Happy smiled an even wider smile than usual when Mr. Birthday admitted that he did not have a clue whose birthday they were all talking about.

"If you come back at three o'clock on Tuesday, then I will tell you whose birthday it is," said Mr. Happy.

By Tuesday, Mr. Birthday was very, very curious.

Have you guessed whose birthday it is yet?

Mr. Birthday turned up at Mr. Happy's house at three o'clock on the dot.

"You have got to tell me now!" burst out Mr. Birthday when Mr. Happy opened the door.

"With pleasure," grinned Mr. Happy. "It is . . ."